How to Live on Practically Nothing a Year

HOW TO LIVE ON PRACTICALLY NOTHING A YEAR

F. SCOTT FITZGERALD

COSIMOCLASSICS

NEW YORK

How to Live on Practically Nothing a Year
Originally published on September 20, 1924 in *The Saturday Evening Post*,
New York
This edition published by Cosimo Classics in 2023

Cover copyright © 2023 by Cosimo, Inc.
Cover image, sketch of F. Scott Fitzgerald, by William Saphier, before 1921.
Sourced from Wikimedia Commons, *https://commons.wikimedia.org/wiki/
File:Sketch_of_F_Scott_Fitzgerald.png*
Cover design by www.heatherkern.com
Interior design by Jeannine C. Ford

ISBN: 978-1-64679-551-2

Ordering Information:
Cosimo publications are available at online bookstores. They may also be
purchased for educational, business, or promotional use:
Bulk orders: Special discounts are available on bulk orders for reading groups,
organizations, businesses, and others.
Custom-label orders: We offer selected books with your customized cover or
logo of choice.

For more information, contact us at www.cosimobooks.com.

How to Live on Practically Nothing a Year

"All right," I said hopefully, "what did it come to for the month?" "Two thousand three hundred and twenty dollars and eighty-two cents." It was the fifth of five long months during which we had tried by every device we knew of to bring the figure of our expenditures safely below the figure of our income. We had succeeded in buying less clothes, less food and fewer luxuries; in fact we had succeeded in everything except in saving money.

"Let's give up," said my wife gloomily. "Look, here's another bill I haven't even opened."

"It isn't a bill; it's got a French stamp."

It was a letter. I read it aloud, and when I finished we looked at each other in a wild, expectant way.

"I don't see why everybody doesn't come over here," it said. "I am now writing from a little inn in France where I just had a meal fit for a king, washed down with champagne, for the absurd sum of sixty-one cents. It costs about one-tenth as much to live over here. From where I sit I can see the smoky peaks of the Alps rising behind a town that was old before Alexander the Great was born…"

By the time we had read the letter for the third time we were in our car bound for New York. As we rushed into the steamship office half an hour later, overturning a rolltop desk and bumping an office boy up against the wall, the agent looked up with mild surprise.

Off to the Riviera to Economize

"Don't utter a word," he said. "You're the twelfth this morning and I understand. You've just got a letter from a friend in Europe telling you how cheap everything is and you want to sail right away. How many?"

"One child," we told him breathlessly.

"Good!" he exclaimed, spreading out a deck of cards on his flat table. "The suits read that you are going on a long, unexpected journey, that you have illness ahead of you and that you will soon meet a number of dark men and women who mean you no good."

As we threw him heavily from the window his voice floated up to us from somewhere between the sixteenth story and the street:

"You sail one week from tomorrow."

Now when a family goes abroad to economize, they don't go to the Wembley exhibition or the Olympic games; in fact they don't go to London and Paris at all, but hasten to the Riviera, which is the southern coast of France and which is reputed to be the cheapest as well as the most beautiful locality in the world. Moreover we were going to the Riviera out of season, which is something like going to Palm Beach for July.

When the Riviera season finishes in late spring, all the wealthy British and American move up to Deauville and Trouville, and all the gambling houses and fashionable milliners and jewelers and second-story men close up their establishments and follow their quarry north. Immediately prices fall. The native Riverans, who have been living on rice and fish all winter, come out of their caves and buy a bottle of red wine and splash about for a bit in their own blue sea.

For two reformed spendthrifts, the Riviera in summer had exactly the right sound. So we put our house in the hands of six real-estate agents and steamed off to France amid the deafening applause of a crowd of friends on the pier—both of whom waved wildly until we were out of sight.

We felt that we had escaped from extravagance and clamor and from all the wild extremes among which we had dwelt for five hectic years, from the tradesman who laid for us and the nurse who bullied us and the couple who kept our house for us and knew us all too well. We were going to the Old World to find a new rhythm for our lives, with a true conviction that we had left our old selves behind forever—and with a capital of just over seven thousand dollars.

The sun coming through high French windows woke us one week later. Outside we could hear the high, clear honk of strange auto horns and we remembered that we were in Paris.

The baby was already sitting up in her cot, ringing the bells which summoned the different fonctionnaires of the hotel as though she had determined to start the day immediately. It was indeed her day, for we were in Paris for no other reason than to get her a nurse.

"Entrez!" we shouted together as there was a knock at the door.

The Governess We Did Not Engage

A handsome waiter opened it and stepped inside, whereupon our child ceased her harmonizing upon the bells and regarded him with marked disfavor.

"Iss a mademoiselle who waited out in the street," he remarked.

"Speak French," I said sternly. "We're all French here."

He spoke French for some time.

"All right," I interrupted after a moment. "Now say that again very slowly in English; I didn't quite understand."

"His name's Entrez," remarked the baby helpfully.

"Be that as it may," I flared up, "his French strikes me as very bad."

We discovered finally that an English-governess was outside to answer our advertisement in the paper.

"Tell her to come in."

After an interval, a tall, languid person in a Rue de la Paix hat strolled into the room and we tried to look as dignified as is possible when sitting up in bed.

"You're Americans ?" she said, seating herself with scornful care.

"Yes."

"I understand you want a nurse. Is this the child?"

"Yes, ma'am."

Here is some high-born lady of the English court, we thought, in temporarily reduced circumstances.

"I've had a great deal of experience," she said, advancing upon our child and attempting unsuccessfully to take her hand. "I'm practically a trained nurse; I'm a lady born and I never complain."

"Complain of what?" demanded my wife.

The applicant waved her hand vaguely.

"Oh, the food, for example."

"Look here," I asked suspiciously, "before we go any farther, let me ask what salary you've been getting."

"For you," she hesitated, "one hundred dollars a month."

"Oh, you wouldn't have to do the cooking too," we assured her; "it's just to take care of one child."

She arose and adjusted her feather boa with fine scorn.

"You'd better get a French nurse," she said, "if you're that kind of people. She won't open the windows at night and your baby will never learn the French word for 'tub, ' but you'll only have to pay her ten dollars a month."

"Good-by," we said together.

"I'll come for fifty."

"Good-by," we repeated.

"For forty—and I'll do the baby's washing."

"We wouldn't take you for your board."

The hotel trembled slightly as she closed the door.

"Where's the lady gone?" asked our child.

"She's hunting Americans," we said. "She looked in the hotel register and thought she saw Chicago written after our names."

We are always witty like that with the baby. She considers us the most amusing couple she has ever known.

The Hot, Sweet South of France

After breakfast I went to the Paris branch of our American bank to get money; but I had no sooner entered it than I wished myself at the hotel, or at least that I had gone in by the back way, for I had evidently been recognized and an enormous crowd began to gather outside. The crowd grew, and I considered going to the window and making them a speech; but I thought that might only increase the disturbance, so I looked around intending to ask someone's advice. I recognized no one, however, except one of the bank officials and a Mr. and Mrs. Douglas Fairbanks from America, who were buying francs at a counter in the rear. So I decided not to show myself; and by the time I had cashed my check the crowd had given up and melted away.

I think now that we did well to get away from Paris in nine days, which, after all, was only a week more than we had intended. Every morning a new boatload of Americans poured into the boulevards, and every afternoon our room at the hotel was filled with familiar faces until— except that there was no faint taste of wood alcohol in the refreshments—we might have been in New York. But at last, with six thousand five hundred dollars remaining, and with an English nurse whom we engaged for twenty-six dollars a month, we boarded the train for the Riviera, the hot, sweet South of France.

When your eyes first fall upon the Mediterranean you know at once why it was here that man first stood erect and stretched out his arms toward the sun. It is a blue sea; or rather it is too blue for that hackneyed phrase which has described every muddy pool from pole to pole. It is the fairy blue of Maxfield Parrish's pictures; blue like blue books, blue oil, blue eyes, and in the shadow of the mountains a green belt of land runs along the coast for a hundred miles and makes a playground for the world. The Riviera! The names of its resorts, Cannes, Nice, Monte Carlo, call up the memory of a hundred kings and princes who have lost their thrones and come here to die, of mysterious rajahs and beys flinging blue diamonds to English dancing girls, of Russian millionaires tossing away fortunes at roulette in the lost caviar days before the war.

From Charles Dickens to Catherine de' Medici, from Prince Edward of Wales in the height of his popularity, to Oscar Wilde in the depth of Jus disgrace, the whole world has come here to forget or to rejoice, to hide its face or have its fling, to build white palaces out of the spoils of oppression or to write the books which sometimes batter those palaces down. Under striped awnings beside the sea grand dukes and gamblers and diplomats and noble courtesans and Balkan czars smoked their slow cigarettes while 1913 drifted into 1914 without a quiver of the calendar, and the fury gathered in the north that was to sweep three-fourths of them away.

Floundering in Flawless French

We reached Hyeres, the town of our destination, in the blazing noon, aware immediately of the tropic's breath as it oozed out of the massed pines. A cabby with a large egg-shaped carbuncle in the center of his forehead struggled with a uniformed hotel porter for the possession of our grips.

"Je suis a stranger here," I said in flawless French. "Je veux aller to le best hotel dans le town."

The porter pointed to an imposing autobus in the station drive.

"Which is the best?" I asked.

For answer, he picked up our heaviest grip, balanced it a moment in his hand, hit the cabby a crashing blow on the forehead—I immediately understood the gradual growth of the carbuncle—and then pressed us firmly toward the car. I tossed several nickels—or rather francs—upon the prostrate carbuncular man.

"Isn't it hot," remarked the nurse.

"I like it very much indeed," I responded, mopping my forehead and attempting a cool smile. I felt that the moral responsibility was with me. I had picked out Hyeres for no more reason than that a friend had once spent a winter there. Besides, we hadn't come here to keep cool; we had come here to economize, to live on practically nothing a year.

"Nevertheless, it's hot," said my wife, and a moment later the child shouted, "Coat off!" in no uncertain voice.

"He must think we want to see the town," I said when, after driving for a mile along a palm-lined road, we stopped in an ancient Mexican-looking square. "Hold on!"

This last was in alarm, for he was hurriedly disembarking our baggage in front of a dilapidated quick-lunch emporium.

"Is this a joke?" I demanded. "Did I tell you to go to the best hotel in town?"

"Here it is," he said.

"No, it isn't. This is the worst hotel I ever saw."

"I am the proprietor," he said.

"I'm sorry, but we've got a baby here"—the nurse obligingly held up the baby—"and we want a more modern hotel, with a bath."

"We have a bath."

"I mean a private bath."

"We will not use while you are here. All the big hotels have shut up themselves for during the summer."

"I don't believe him for a minute," said my wife.

I looked around helplessly. Two scanty, hungry women had come out of the door and were looking voraciously at our baggage. Suddenly I heard the sound of slow hoofs, and glancing up I beheld the carbuncular man driving disconsolately up the dusty street.

"What's le best hotel dans le town?" I shouted at him.

"Non, non, non, non!" he cried, waving his reins excitedly. "Jardin Hotel open!"

As the proprietor dropped my grip and started toward the cabby at a run, I turned to the hungry women accusingly.

"What do you mean by having a bus like this?" I demanded.

I felt very American and superior; I intimated that if the morals of the French people were in this decadent state I regretted that we had ever entered the war.

"Daddy's hot too," remarked the baby irrelevantly.

"I am not hot!"

"Daddy had better stop talking and find us a hotel," remarked the English nurse, "before we all melt away."

It was the work of but an hour to pay off the proprietor, to add damages for his wounded feelings and to install ourselves in the Hotel du Jardin, on the edge of town.

"Hyeres," says my guidebook, "is the very oldest and warmest of the Riviera winter resorts and is now frequented almost exclusively by the English."

But when we arrived there late in May, even the

English, except the very oldest and warmest, had moved away. At dinner, only a superannuated dozen, a slowly decaying dozen, a solemn and dispirited dozen remained. But we were to be there merely while we searched for a villa, and it had the advantage of being amazingly cheap for a first class hotel. The rate for four of us, including meals, was one hundred and fifty francs—less than eight dollars a day.

The real-estate agent, an energetic young gentleman with his pants buttoned snugly around his chest, called on us next morning.

"Dozens of villas," he said enthusiastically. "We will take the horse and buggy and go see."

It was a simmering morning, but the streets already swarmed with the faces of Southern France—dark faces, for there is an Arab streak along the Riviera, left from turbulent, forgotten centuries. Once the Moors harried the coast for gain, and later, as they swept up through Spain in mad glory, they threw out frontier towns along the shores as outposts for their conquest of the world. They were not the first people, or the last, that have tried to overrun France. All that remains now for proud Moslem hopes is an occasional Moorish tower and the tragic glint of black Eastern eyes.

"Now this villa rents for thirty dollars a month," said the real-estate agent as we stopped at a small house on the edge of town.

"What's the matter with it?" asked my wife suspiciously.

"Nothing at all. It is superb. It has six rooms and a well."

"A well?"

"A fine well."

"Do you mean it has no bathroom?"

"Not what you would call an actual bathroom."

"Drive on," we said.

It was obvious by noon that there were no villas to be let in Hyeres. Those we saw were all too hot, too small, too duty or too triste, an expressive word which implies that the mad marquis still walk through the halls in his shroud.

"Yes, we have no villas today," remarked the agent, smiling.

"That's a very old played-out joke," I said, "and I am too hot to laugh."

Extracting Information

Our clothes were hanging on us like wet towels, but when I had established our identity by a scar on my left hand we were admitted to the hotel. I decided to ask one of the lingering Englishmen if there was perhaps another quiet town near by.

Now, asking something of an American or a Frenchman is a definite thing: the only difference is that you can understand the American's reply. But getting an answer from an Englishman is about as complicated as borrowing a match from the Secretary of State. The first one I approached dropped his paper, looked at me in horror and bolted precipitately from the room. This disconcerted me for a moment but luckily my eyes fell on a man whom I had seen being wheeled in to dinner.

"Good morning," I said. "Could you tell me—" He jerked spasmodically, but to my relief, he was unable to leave his seat. "I wonder if you know a town where I could get a villa for the summer."

"Don't know any at all," he said coldly. "And I wouldn't tell you if I did."

He didn't exactly pronounce the last sentence, but I could read the words as they issued from his eyes.

"I suppose you're a newcomer too," I suggested.

"I've been here every winter for sixteen years."

Pretending to detect an invitation in this, I drew up my chair.

"Then you must know some town," I assured him.

"Cannes, Nice, Monte Carlo."

"But they're too expensive. I want a quiet place to do a lot of work."

"Cannes, Nice, Monte Carlo. All quiet in summer. Don't know any others. Wouldn't tell you if I did. Good day."

Upstairs, the nurse was counting the mosquito bites on the baby, all received during the night, and my wife was adding them up in a big book.

"Cannes, Nice, Monte Carlo," I said.

"I'm glad we're going to leave this broiling town," remarked the nurse.

"I think we'd better try Cannes."

"I think so too," said my wife eagerly. "I hear it's very gay—I mean, it's no economy to stay where you can't work, and I don't believe we can get a villa here after all."

"Let's go on the big boat," said the baby suddenly.

"Silence! We've come to the Riviera and we're here to stay."

The Villa of Our Dreams

So we decided to leave the nurse and baby in Hyeres and run up to Cannes, which is a more fashionable town in a more northerly situation along the shore. Now when you run up to somewhere you have to have an automobile, so we bought the only new one in town next day. It had the power of six horses—the age of the horses was not stated—and it was so small that we loomed out of it like giants; so small that you could run it under the veranda for the night. It had no lock, no speedometer, no gauge, and its cost, including the parcel-post charge, was seven hundred and fifty dollars. We started for Cannes in it, and except for the warm exhaust when other cars drove over us, we found the trip comparatively cool.

All the celebrities of Europe have spent a season in Cannes; even the Man with the Iron Mask whiled away twelve years on an island off its shore. Its gorgeous villas are built of stone so soft that it is sawed instead of hewed. We looked at four of them next morning. They were small, neat and clean; you could have matched them in any suburb of Los Angeles. They rented at sixty-five dollars a month.

"I like them," said my wife firmly. "Let's rent one. They look awfully easy to run."

"We didn't come abroad to find a house that was easy to run," I objected. "How could I write looking out on a"—I glanced out the window and my eyes met a splendid view of the sea—"where I'd hear every whisper in the house."

So we moved on to the fourth villa, the wonderful fourth villa the memory of which still causes me to lie awake and hope that some bright day will find me there. It rose in white marble out of a great hill, like a chateau, like a castle of old. The very taxicab that took us there had romance in its front seat.

"Did you notice our driver?" said the agent, leaning toward me. "He used to be a Russian millionaire."

We peered through the glass at him—a thin dispirited man who ordered the gears about with a lordly air.

"The town is full of them," said the agent. "They're glad to get jobs as chauffeurs, butlers or waiters. The women work as femmes de chambre in the hotels."

"Why don't they open tea rooms like Americans do?"

"Many of them aren't fit for anything. We're awfully sorry for them, but—" He leaned forward and tapped on the glass. "Would you mind driving a little faster? We haven't got all day."

"Look," he said when we reached the chateau on the hill. "There's the Grand Duke Michael's villa next door."

"You mean he's the butler there?"

"Oh, no; he's got money. He's gone north for the summer."

When we had entered through scrolled brass gates that creaked massively as gates should for a king, and when the blinds had been drawn, we were in a high central hall hung with ancestral portraits of knights in armor and courtiers in satin and brocade. It was like a movie set. Flights of marble stairs rose in solid dignity to form a grand gallery into which light dropped through blue figured glass upon a mosaic floor. It was modern, too, with huge clean beds and a model kitchen and three bathrooms and a solemn, silent study overlooking the sea.

"It belonged to a Russian general," said the agent; "killed in Silesia during the war."

"How much is it?"

"For the summer, one hundred and ten dollars a month."

"Done!" I said. "Fix up the lease right away. My wife will go to Hyeres immediately to get the—"

"Just a minute," she said, frowning. "How many servants will it take to run this house?"

"Why, I should say,"—the agent glanced at us sharply and hesitated—"about five."

"I should say about eight." She turned to me. "Let's go to Newport and rent the Vanderbilt house instead."

"Remember," said the agent, "you've got the Grand Duke Michael on your left."

"Will he come to see us?" I inquired.

"He would, of course," explained the agent, "only, you see, he's gone away."

We held debate upon the mosaic floor. My theory was that I couldn't work in the little houses and that this would be a real investment because of its romantic inspiration. My wife's theory was that eight servants eat a lot of food and that it simply wouldn't do. We apologized to the agent, shook hands respectfully with the millionaire taxi driver and gave him five francs, and in a state of great dejection returned to Hyeres.

"Here's the hotel bill," said my wife as we went despondently in to dinner.

"Thank heaven, its only fifty-five dollars."

I opened it. To my amazement, tax after tax had been added beneath the bill—government tax, city tax, a ten per cent tax to retip the servants.

I looked gloomily at a nameless piece of meat soaked in a lifeless gravy which reclined on my plate.

"I think it's goat's meat," said the nurse, following my eyes. She turned to my wife. "Did you ever taste goat's meat, Mrs. Fitzgerald?"

But Mrs. Fitzgerald had never tasted goat's meat and Mrs. Fitzgerald had fled.

Hunting His Majesty

As I wandered dismally about the hotel next day, hoping that our house on Long Island hadn't been rented so that we could go home for the summer, I noticed that the halls were even more deserted than usual. There seemed to be more old copies of the *Illustrated London News* about, and more empty chairs. At dinner we had the goat again. As I looked around the empty dining room I suddenly realized that the last Englishman had taken his cane and his conscience and fled to London. The management was keeping open a two-hundred-room hotel for us alone!

Hyeres grew warmer and we rested there in a helpless daze. We knew now why Catherine de' Medici had chosen it for her favorite resort. A month of it in the summer and she must have returned to Paris with a dozen St. Bartholomew's sizzling in her head. In vain we took trips to Nice, to Antibes, to St. Maximin—we were worried now; a fourth of our seven thousand had slipped away. Then one morning just five weeks after we had left New York we got off the train at a little town that we had never considered before. It was a red little town built close to the sea, with gay red-roofed houses and an air of repressed carnival about it; carnival that would venture forth into the streets before night. We knew that we would love to live in it and we asked a citizen the whereabouts of the real-estate agency.

"Ah, for that you had far better ask the king," he exclaimed.

A principality! A second Monaco! We had not known there were two of them along the French shore.

"And a bank that will cash a letter of credit?"

"For that, too, you must ask the king."

He pointed the way toward the palace down a long shady street, and my wife hurriedly produced a mirror and began powdering her face.

"But our dusty clothes," I said modestly. "Do you think the king will—"

He considered.

"I'm not sure about clothes," he answered. "But I think—yes, I think the king will attend to that for you too."

I hadn't meant that, but we thanked him and with much inward trepidation proceeded toward the imperial domain. After half an hour, when royal turrets had failed to rise against the sky, I stopped another man.

"Can you tell us the way to the imperial palace?"

"The what?"

"We want to get an interview with his majesty—his majesty the king."

The word "king" caught his attention. His mouth opened understandingly and he pointed to a sign over our heads:

"W. F. King," I read, "Anglo-American Bank, Real-Estate Agency, Railroad Tickets, Insurance, Tours and Excursions, Circulating Library."

Where Things are So Cheap

The potentate turned out to be a brisk, efficient Englishman of middle age who had gradually acquired the little town to himself over a period of twenty years.

"We are Americans come to Europe to economize," I told him. "We've combed the Riviera from Nice to Hyeres and haven't been able to find a villa. Meanwhile our money is leaking gradually away."

He leaned back and pressed a button and almost immediately a lean, gaunt woman appeared in the door.

"This is Marthe," he said, "your cook."

We could hardly believe our ears.

"Do you mean you have a villa for us?"

"I have already selected one," he said. "My agents saw you getting off the train."

He pressed another button and a second woman stood respectfully beside the first.

"This is Jeanne, your femme de chambre. She does the mending, too, and waits on the table. You pay her thirteen dollars a month and you pay Marthe sixteen dollars. Marthe does the marketing, however, and expects to make a little on the side for herself."

"But the villa?"

"The lease is being made out now. The price is seventy-nine dollars a month and your check is good with me. We move you in tomorrow."

Within an hour we had seen our home, a clean cool villa set in a large garden on a hill above town. It was what we had been looking for all along. There was a summerhouse and a sand pile and two bathrooms and roses for breakfast and a gardener who called me milord.

When we had paid the rent, only thirty-five hundred dollars, half our original capital, remained. But we felt that at last we could begin to live on practically nothing a year.

In the late afternoon of September 1, 1924, a distinguished-looking young man, accompanied by a young lady might have been seen lounging on a sandy beach in France. Both of them were burned to a deep chocolate brown, so that at first they seemed to be of Egyptian origin; but closer inspection showed that their faces had an Aryan cast and that their voices, when they spoke, had a faintly nasal, North American ring. Near them played a small black child with cotton-white hair who from time to time beat a tin spoon upon a pail and shouted, "Regardez-moi!" in no uncertain voice.

Out of the casino near by drifted weird rococo music—a song dealing with the non-possession of a specific yellow fruit in a certain otherwise well—stocked store. Waiters, both Senegalese and European, rushed around among the bathers with many-colored drinks, pausing now and then to chase away the children of the poor, who were dressing and undressing with neither modesty nor self-consciousness, upon the sand.

"Hasn't it been a good summer!" said the young man lazily. "We've become absolutely French."

"And the French are such an aesthetic people," said the young lady, listening for a moment to the banana music. "They know how to live. Think of all the nice things they have to eat!"

"Delicious things! Heavenly things!" exclaimed the young man, spreading some American deviled ham on some biscuits marked Springfield, Illinois. "But then they've studied the food question for two thousand years."

"And things are so cheap here!" cried the young lady enthusiastically. "Think of perfume! Perfume that would cost fifteen dollars in New York, you can get here for five."

The young man struck a Swedish match and lit an American cigarette.

"The trouble with most Americans in France," he remarked sonorously, "is that they won't lead a real French life. They hang around the big hotels and exchange opinions fresh from the States."

"I know," she agreed. "That's exactly what it said in the *New York Times* this morning."

The American music ended and the English nurse arose, implying that it was time the child went home to supper. With a sigh, the young man arose, too, and shook himself violently, scattering a great quantity of sand.

"We've got to stop on the way and get some Arizon-oil gasoline," he said. "That last stuff was awful."

"The check, suh," said a Senegalese waiter with an accent from well below the Mason-Dixon Line. "That'll be ten francs fo' two glasses of beer."

The young man handed him the equivalent of seventy cents in the gold-colored hat checks of France. Beer was perhaps a little higher than in America, but then he had had the privilege of hearing the historic banana song on a real, or almost real, jazz band. And waiting for him at home was a regular French supper-baked beans from the quaint old Norman town of Akron, Ohio, an omelet fragrant with la Chicago bacon and a cup of English tea.

But perhaps you have already recognized in these two cultured Europeans the same barbaric Americans who had left America just five months before; and perhaps you wonder that the change could have come about so quickly. The secret is that they had entered fully into the life of the Old World. Instead of patronizing tourist hotels they had made excursions to quaint little out-of-the-way restaurants, with the real French atmosphere, where supper for two rarely came to more than ten or fifteen dollars. Not for them the glittering capitals—Paris, Brussels, Rome.

They were content with short trips to beautiful historic old towns, such as Monte Carlo, where they once left their automobile with a kindly garage man who paid their hotel bill and bought them tickets home.

The High Cost of Economizing

Yes, our summer had been a complete success. And we had lived on practically nothing—that is, on practically nothing except our original seven thousand dollars. It was all gone.

The trouble is that we had come to the Riviera out of season—that is, out of one season, but in the middle of another. For in summer the people who are trying to economize come South, and the shrewd French know that this class is the very easiest game of all, as people who are trying to get something for nothing are very liable to be.

Exactly where the money went we don't know—we never do. There were the servants, for example. I was very fond of Marthe and Jeanne—and afterwards of their sisters Eugenie and Serpolette, who came in to help—but on my own initiative it would never have occurred to me to insure them all. Yet that was the law. If Jeanne suffocated in her mosquito netting, if Marthe tripped over a bone and broke her thumb, I was responsible. I wouldn't have minded so much except that the little on the side that Marthe made in doing our marketing amounted, as I figure, to about forty-five per cent.

Our weekly bills at the grocer's and the butcher's averaged sixty-five dollars, or higher than they had ever been in an expensive Long Island town. Whatever the meat actually cost, it was almost invariably inedible; while as for the milk, every drop of it had to be boiled, because the cows were tubercular in France. For fresh vegetables we had tomatoes and a little asparagus; that was all—the only garlic that can be put over on us must be administered in sleep. I wondered often how the Riviera middle class—the bank clerk, say, who supports a family on from forty to seventy dollars a month—manages to keep alive.

"It's even worse in winter," a little French girl told us on the beach. "The English and Americans drive the prices up until we can't buy and we don't know what to do. My sister had to go to Marseilles and find work, and she's only fourteen. Next winter I'll go too."

No Money and No Regrets

There simply isn't enough to go around; and the Americans who, because of their own high standard of material comfort, want the best obtainable, naturally have to pay. And in addition, the sharp French tradesmen are always ready to take advantage of a careless American eye.

"I don't like this bill," I said to the food-and-ice deliverer. "I arranged to pay you five francs and not eight francs a day."

He became unintelligible for a moment to gain time.

"My wife added it up," he said.

Those valuable Riviera wives! Always they are adding up their husbands' accounts, and the dear ladies simply don't know one figure from another. Such a talent in the wife of a railroad president would be an asset worth many million dollars.

It is twilight as I write this, and out of my window darkening banks of trees, set one clump behind another in many greens, slope down to the evening sea. The flaming sun has collapsed behind the peaks of the Esterels and the moon already hovers over the Roman aqueducts of Frejus, five miles away. In half an hour Rene and Bobbe, officers of aviation, are coming to dinner in their white ducks; and Rene, who is only twenty-three and has never recovered from having missed the war, will tell us romantically how he wants to smoke opium in Peking and how he writes a few things "for myself alone." Afterwards, in the garden, their white uniforms will grow dimmer as the more liquid dark comes down, until they, like the heavy roses and the nightingales in the pines, will seem to take an essential and indivisible part in the beauty of this proud gay land.

And though we have saved nothing, we have danced the carmagnole; and, except for the day when my wife took the mosquito lotion for a mouth wash, and the time when I tried to smoke a French cigarette, and, as Ring Lardner would say, swooned, we haven't yet been sorry that we came.

The dark-brown child is knocking at the door to bid me good night.

"Going on the big boat, daddy?" she says in broken English.

"No."

"Why?"

"Because we're going to try it for another year, and besides—think of perfume!"

We are always like that with the baby. She considers us the wittiest couple she has ever known.

COSIMO

COSIMO is a specialty publisher of books and publications that inspire, inform, and engage readers. Our mission is to offer unique books to niche audiences around the world.

COSIMO BOOKS publishes books and publications for innovative authors, nonprofit organizations, and businesses. **COSIMO BOOKS** specializes in bringing books back into print, publishing new books quickly and effectively, and making these publications available to readers around the world.

COSIMO CLASSICS offers a collection of distinctive titles by the great authors and thinkers throughout the ages. At **COSIMO CLASSICS** timeless works find new life as affordable books, covering a variety of subjects including: Business, Economics, History, Personal Development, Philosophy, Religion & Spirituality, and much more!

COSIMO REPORTS publishes public reports that affect your world, from global trends to the economy, and from health to geopolitics.

FOR MORE INFORMATION CONTACT US AT
INFO@COSIMOBOOKS.COM

➢ if you are a book lover interested in our current catalog of books

➢ if you represent a bookstore, book club, or anyone else interested in special discounts for bulk purchases

➢ if you are an author who wants to get published

➢ if you represent an organization or business seeking to publish books and other publications for your members, donors, or customers.

**COSIMO BOOKS ARE ALWAYS
AVAILABLE AT ONLINE BOOKSTORES**

VISIT COSIMOBOOKS.COM
BE INSPIRED, BE INFORMED

Milton Keynes UK
Ingram Content Group UK Ltd.
UKHW040311080224
437360UK00001B/21

9 781646 795512